I0638800

Animal Eyes

and

Other Stories

Animal Eyes

and

Other Stories

Elizabeth Devido

REDHAWK
PUBLICATIONS

Copyright © 2022 Elizabeth Devido

ISBN: 978-1-952485-38-1

Published by
Redhawk Publications
The Catawba Valley Community College Press
2550 US Hwy 70 SE
Hickory NC 28602

All rights reserved, including the right to reproduce this book or portions thereof in any form whatsoever. For information, address the publisher.

Contents

Henry Sees A Ghost

My best friend Henry lived next to a cemetery. From the time we were little kids, growing up on different sides of town, it became our go-to place for whatever nonsense we could come up with. Every day after school, the two of us would bike down to his house to play amongst the tombstones.

The cemetery became a place that was just for us. Neither Henry nor I had a lot of friends. He was the class clown who took delight in pissing people off with his pranks. I was the quiet kid who stuttered whenever he was asked to speak. At school, we were ignored, but at the cemetery, we could be ghosts, zombies, vampires, anything other than two weirdos at the back of the class.

Henry was always the one suggesting we do crazy stuff. I was never much of a risk-taking person, so I relied on Henry to get me out of my shell. If it wasn't for him, I'd probably stay at home all the time. A week before graduation, he dragged me out to the creek at three a.m. to swim near an alligators' nest. Got my hair caught in some branches just over the water and had to pull a chunk of hair out to escape before the gators smelled us. That's not the kind of thing I would have done if Henry hadn't pushed me.

The craziest thing Henry ever did was tell me he could see ghosts. He told me he'd look out his window and see specters wandering the cemetery. A civil war soldier who got his head blown off by a cannon. A teenage girl who died by suicide, her mouth still foaming from all the pills she took. A man in a jumpsuit who was sentenced to death for a crime he didn't commit. Sometimes when we hung out around the tombs, he would get really quiet all of a sudden and look around like someone else had spoken to him.

I always figured Henry was just exaggerating. Putting on a show just to scare me. I wasn't a brave kid, but I didn't believe in ghosts.

I didn't realize he was dead serious until the night we went grave-robbing.

We were seventeen. Our senior year was over, and Henry wanted us to end high school with something wild before college sent us to opposite sides of the country. His plan was stupid-crazy in the way only an idea conjured by Henry could be: Dig up some graves in the cemetery and steal whatever we could find that the local pawn shop would take. One of our favorite games to play as kids was pretend graverobbers, and taking out the pretend part would bring it full circle. The conversation that followed went how most conversations between me and Henry did: I called him an idiot, told him it was a bad idea, then ultimately gave in when he called me a coward.

After our final day of classes, Henry and I drove down to the cemetery. Henry parked his truck by his house, and after grabbing a shovel from his back shed, we slumped down the hill into the cluster of tombstones. It was already getting dark out, and Henry had to use the flashlight on his phone to make sure we didn't trip on anything.

As we walked, Henry's usual chattiness started to wane. You'd think considering this was his idea that he wouldn't shut up. But as soon as we began navigating the stones and bushes, he stopped talking.

"You seeing a ghost?" I chuckled.

He didn't respond. He kept his eyes ahead until we were near the other end of the cemetery. The sun had set enough that the sky was dark blue, and I could barely read any of the headstones anymore.

"This one," Henry said. He stopped at a headstone just below a bush. Then he tossed the shovel to me. "I'll hold the light, you dig."

I was about to remind him that this was his idea and so he should be the one digging, but I saw the light from the phone reflect on Henry's eyes. The eagerness he had before was drained out, and I couldn't tell what had replaced it.

Whatever. I wanted us to get out of there before the grounds-keeper found us. I pressed the shovel into the earth where Henry aimed the light and started digging.

By the time I was six feet in, it was nearly pitch black out, and my sweaty shirt was sticking to my back. The tip of the shovel hit something hard, and a sleek white coffin appeared under the dirt.

"Jackpot," I said.

I looked at Henry. I expected him to be excited. But he was quiet and looking at me with an expression I couldn't read.

"You open it," he said.

He said it coldly, like it wasn't a suggestion. I turned to the coffin and cracked it open. For a body that was supposedly buried with valuable objects, the family did a crappy job keeping it locked up tight.

I opened the lid.

Inside there were no heirloom jewels, no precious items, no expensive clothes. Henry's light traced over a familiar suit and head of red hair. A pale face too fresh to be long dead.

I turned to look at Henry again. I waited for the punchline. I waited for him to fall into hysterics. I waited for him to tell me I should see the look on my face. But his face was stone-still without a trace of his usual humor.

"Henry," I said.

"You really don't remember at all, do you?"

"Remember what, exactly?"

"Our swim down at the gator creek last week. You got stuck underwater...your hair...I couldn't...didn't get it unstuck in time."

"The hell are you going on about?"

"I lied, Carter. I didn't bring you here to steal anything. I...I wanted to show you because you won't go away."

I looked back down at the body. In the skull, I could see a bald spot, a place where a tuft of hair had been ripped out. I felt cold all of a sudden, like the creek water had found its way back around me.

I couldn't remember going home that night. I couldn't remember pulling myself onto the shore. One minute I was underwater, and everything after...just murky.

"I never said anything because I didn't want you to go," Henry said. "But it was my idea to take you to the creek...so I thought I would be the one to see you out of the earth."

I expected to shake, but for the first time, I was aware that my body couldn't seem to shiver. Because it was looking up at me from the hole below. Up above I could hear Henry sniffle. My best friend never cried. In the face of everything, he always made jokes. But I could feel the tears trickling down my best friend's cheeks.

When I brought my eyes back up, he wasn't there anymore. All that looked back at me was a sky full of stars, getting brighter and brighter.

Red Paint Puddle

My father has not left the basement in seven days. In any other circumstances, this would not be unusual. Since my parents moved into our family abode the year I was born, the basement has served as my father's art studio. Take a look around down there and you'll find all his favorite pieces: Dollhouses with immaculately tiled roofs and brick-by-brick walls. Models of new property developments complete with little cars in the parking lots and signs in the windows. Hotels, gardens, train tracks, national parks, and monuments. Each of them so detailed you could see splinters in the wood, grass sprouting in cracks in the concrete, dimples on the miniature people that walk the foam grounds.

All of my father's work focused on small things. He could paint freckles on his little miniature dolls, create details so small you'd need a microscope to see them. My mother used to tease him about how he could only understand the world through a bird's eye view. The world was easier to understand when it was small enough to fit on a display. Patrons could spend hours squinting at my father's dioramas and never run out of hidden details to find.

Lots of different people found my father's talents useful. Property developers who needed models of the hotels and shopping malls they wanted to build. Museums that needed dioramas of civil war battlefields complete with little uniformed soldiers. Toy shops that wanted to sell his handmade dollhouses. But my father's favorite works were always his nature dioramas. Nothing kept him in a trance like creating the natural world with man-made materials. He could paint microscopic veins on leaves the size of fingernails, make tiny anthills on brown-painted dirt, cake rocks with mud and shiny water.

My father has been working on one of these nature dioramas for the past few weeks. All this time he's forsaken the outside world to build his own within the deepest walls in the house. When he gets to the end of a project, it takes a lot to pull him from his studio to eat dinner. But I haven't seen him once. He hasn't stopped once.

He hasn't stopped since my mother left us.

—

The project began over a year ago, after a camping trip that left our family one member short. I had just graduated from our local college and my mother insisted we celebrate with a trek up in the mountains. We packed the needed supplies and set up a tent just a few miles hike from a stream.

It was my mother's idea for us to go fishing on the first day. While my father enjoyed recreating the outdoors, my mother loved living in it. She loved to dig her hands in the earth until the soil stuck under her fingernails. She loved to wet her socks in the lake, catch fish with her bare hands. The moment our tent was ready, she pulled out three fishing poles.

"If we leave for the river now, we can grab a few in time for dinner," she said, then gave me a wink. "We'll catch ourselves some grub."

"You go ahead," my father said. He tossed his sleeping bag inside the tent. "We still have more stuff to unload from the car." It was his turn to look at me. "Clarice, can you help me?"

I was about to refuse until my mother answered for me.

"I'll go set up the poles by the water," she said. "I hear there's a rocky bridge over the stream. I want to check it out before we start. I'll be up there when you're ready."

She gave me a wink then disappeared down the path with three fishing pools swinging over her shoulder. I didn't think much of it. I did as my father said as we unloaded the rest of our supplies. I moved quickly because I wanted to see the bridge my mother mentioned. At one point, my father handed me a stack of wooden logs.

"I'm going to go check on mom," my father said. "Set these a few feet from the tent. We'll need it to boil hotdogs later."

I watched my father disappear down the same hiking path my mother took. The sun was starting its descent and the air in the mountains was growing cold and crisp. I arranged the logs the way my father taught me in trips past. I kept them a safe distance from the tent so none of our things would burn.

The task was a bit tedious, and I was impatiently waiting to go to the stream to fish. The woods were quiet, hardly any animals were heard. So when I heard footsteps running down the path, along with my father's uneven breathing, I immediately sensed something was wrong.

My father reemerged from the path.

"Dad," I said. I dropped the log I was holding and made my way towards him. "Something wrong?"

He stopped me before I could approach the path.

"Don't go to the river," he said between sharp inhales. "Don't... your mother..." He gave me a watery look, one I'd never seen on my father before. "She...wasn't on the bridge...she was...I found her in the water. She...I think she fell." He placed his shaking hands on my arms. "She hit her head on a boulder...she's not moving...I found her in the water..."

———

I come home from work and turn into the hallway stretching between the entryway and the kitchen. My footsteps trail down floorboards older than me. On most days, my first stop after work is to grab dinner in the kitchen. But I decided today I will finally check on my father.

The basement door sticks out against the pale wallpaper like a stain. I've walked past that doorway every day, coming to and from work, for weeks now. Right at my feet is this morning's breakfast for papa. Not a single bite eaten.

The door opens silently, without a single creak. Despite the age of this house, everything is quiet enough that anyone could walk around without making a sound. I'm greeted with a waft of smells from the top of the stairs. It's been so long since I've been in the basement that the smell is almost nostalgic: Oil and paint, leather shoes, and cigarettes.

I drop down step by step, and I'm quiet so as not to startle my father. The basement is lit by a single lightbulb hanging from a beady string. The light is as oily and yellow as a rotted tooth. My eyes look for my father.

It doesn't take long to find him.

My father is not hunched over on his old bar stool. His thin spine is snapped over the table. He's collapsed on the floor, crunched up on the carpet with his hands to his throat. The carpet by his mouth is caked with dried vomit.

My heart hitches in my throat, and the silence of the house screams at me. I stumble forward onto my knees right by my father's body. *Corpse. Cadaver.* Those words pass through my head, but I refuse to hear them.

My hands shake over my father. I can't bring myself to touch him. I fear if I do, his body will crumble to dust. I kneel on the floor. My body is too quiet and too loud. My mind scrambles the scene around me, looking for answers. I look at the vomit by his lips, then run my eyes down his arm, and to the uncapped paint tube in his hand.

Suicide. Toxic chemicals in the paints, the ones he used to create the individual stripes on penny-sized butterflies, had poisoned him. Whatever had taken over my father, that locked him away in this house, decided to end it all with his favorite material.

It feels like centuries later before I tear my eyes away from my father. I lift my gaze as if I could find something in the room that could revive him. But the only thing the light in the room touches is the diorama on the table. I rise to my feet and look over it.

My father has been working on it for months, and it's one of the most impressive pieces I've seen of his. The plastic stream that runs across the piece seems to stir with murk. The trees are bare, and each hair-thin branch is speckled with details. It's new. Some of the paint looks like it hasn't even dried yet.

The scene is a simple one: A murky stream running from one end of the display to the next, passing under a hole in a cliff, and bordered by a cluster of leafless trees and bushes. The rocky structure of the cliff is pigmented with grey, orange, and white layers of rock. The twigs blur together in a fuzz of rust. No flowers, no animals, no brightly glittering leaves. There's only one bright color in the diorama, and it's a spot of red in the river.

There are two miniature figurines: One stands on the rocky bridge stretched high over the stream. I lean over the table and squint to get a better look. The man on the bridge is dark-haired, dressed in a green flannel complete with orange and red stripes. His jeans look like real denim, and his shoes have tiny shoelaces. His gaze bends over the edge, and his face is painted with round eyes and an open mouth.

My gaze follows down with his, to the red spot on the water. The second figurine is half-submerged in the plastic stream, face down, her blonde hair sprawled in the waves. The red paint spills into the water, running from her head to a boulder right by the water's edge.

The scene squirms in my stomach, before I can even remember what—who—is on the floor behind me. My father's dioramas were always pleasant to look at, but they never contained stories. The families in his dollhouses were happily seated at their little dining room tables, the museum soldier figurines lined neatly in a row. Even his Civil War recreations had very little bloodshed. Nothing like this.

My hands shake and fumble as I reach for my father's magnifying glass, kept alongside his row of thin brushes. I hover over the figurines, watching their tiny features grow under the shiny glass.

They're glued to the plastic ecosystem around them, a perfect recreation of...a mountain? A park? A...

Camping ground.

The words enter my ears as if someone had whispered them. Both figurines are wearing little backpacks I've seen before. I see the man on the rocky overreach, high above the little trees, looking down at the woman in the water. His expression is shocked, his mouth is wide, and he looks exactly like the man on the floor behind me.

And the woman. Her face is down in the water. Even my father may have not bothered to paint her face on. But I know those short blonde curls, that purple shirt, and white hiking shorts. The running shoes with the bright pink shoelaces...

My eyes fall to a small plaque at the front of the display. The title is one word: ACCIDENT.

Ghostwriter

I've only ever seen Mitchell Decker's house in photos. The two-story block of white columns and black shutters just a stone's throw outside of Portland, Maine, sits nestled in the trees. A couple of rain clouds are starting to form by the time I pull up to the house and the autumn trees are stark. It's exactly the kind of place I'd expect to meet the creator of Dominic Black.

I've only brought one suitcase with me for my stay here: My laptop, notebook and pen, and the first copy of *Dominic Black: Thicker Than Blood* I ever bought. The one still scribbled with my dad's annotations from long before I was born, mixed in with a few of my own. The copy is older than me, with yellowing pages and writing in the margins. I'm going to need it for the next couple of months.

I ring the doorbell and it echoes on the other side. I expect Decker to answer, assuming he's well enough to walk. A moment later, the door opens to reveal a lady in a beige uniform and an auburn bun piled on top of her head. Mitchell Decker she is not.

"Daniel Armstrong, right?" she says.

I give her a grin and a nod.

"That would be me," I say.

"Perfect punctuality," she says with a grin. "Amelia Rhodes. I'm Mr. Decker's at-home hospice caretaker. You and I are going to be staying here together for a while."

She holds open the door for me and I step inside. The interior of the house looks exactly like the ones in Decker's novels. A spiral staircase leads up past a chandelier to the second floor. I follow Amelia up and towards a room down the hall. I'm shaking enough that I can feel it in my bones.

Amelia taps her knuckles on the door.

"Mr. Decker," she says. "Our ghostwriter is here."

A horse, muffled voice answers from the other side. Amelia turns to smile at me, then opens the door for me to step inside.

The room smells like a variety of unidentifiable chemicals. Orange pill containers ar scattered about the room. A variety of tubes and shiny medical supplies. In the middle of it all is Mitchell Decker, propped up in his bed by a pillow on his lower back. He turns his eyes to me and I'm sweating.

"Mr. Armstrong," he says. "Glad to see the nasty weather didn't slow you down."

"Trust me, sir, Mother Nature's going to have to try a lot harder to keep me from coming here."

Decker gestures to a seat across from the bed, and I take a seat while Amelia examines the medicine bottles on the table.

"Thank you, again, sir, for the opportunity," I say. I set my suitcase down next to me. "And thank you for letting me stay here.

Landlord's been a pain in the ass. It's nice to get away to focus on a project as huge as this."

"I'm sure it is." Decker laces his fingers on his lap. "I guess the first order of business is logistics. You'll be staying in the guest room for as long as it takes to complete the manuscript. You'll be working off the plans I've already written out. Once you think the final novel is satisfactory, I'll read over it, and we'll decide together if it's ready to show the publisher. Sound good?"

I nod.

"As for writing credits," he continues. "You are not permitted to speak of any details of the book until it is released."

"Of course, sir," I say. Then I whisper conspiratorially, "And make sure no one knows the book is ghostwritten."

He grins and nods with a chuckle.

"If I were asking you to write a few more books, I might've requested your name on the cover. But since this final book is a bit unexpected due to sudden circumstances…" He gestures to the tube at his nose and the two of us giggle. "…the publisher wants just my name. It's an author brand issue. But I can promise you'll be properly compensated for your work."

"Writing a Dominic Black book is damn near compensation enough. I've been reading these books since I could read chapter books. My dad had all the earlier editions of the first books from the eighties."

"Your dad had good taste. Love those old pulpy covers."

Decker sits up in bed. He lets out a grunt, and I think I hear something pop. The first time I saw him was in an author photo in the back of my dad's copy of the third book, *Dominic Black: Six Feet Under*. A man with silvered black hair and a gold tooth at the front of his mouth. His hair's all white now and his back is bent from years crunched over a desk. He's still got that gold tooth though.

"If you'd like to look over my notes this evening, so you can get started tomorrow," He reaches for the nightstand. Amelia opens the drawer and hands him a thin stack of stapled papers. He thanks her, then hands the stack to me. "Here's the outline of the whole thing. Look over it tonight. If you have any other ideas or tweaks you think would help, let me know by tomorrow before you get started."

It took all my willpower not to snatch it from his hand.

"Will do, sir. Thank you."

—

My first night at the house, I settle into an overstuffed chair in the guest room with the outline on my lap. It's only a few pages long. The text is divided into chapters with bullet points outlining the events and important details, leaving empty space to add my own embellishments. My hot tea on the nightstand goes cold as I tear through it. I feel like a kid opening his presents before Christmas morning.

At around eleven, I flip over to the last page. My eyes wander down the page to the last section labeled "Chapter 47." My heart jerks and tugs in my chest.

Then collapses in my ribcage.

I read over the line several times. I check for typos, some sign that there was a mistake, some mishap in the printing or the word processing program. But my eyes read the last sentence over and over until the words don't say anything anymore:

Dominic is taken back to the motel following the heroin injection. His wife holds his hand (the beeping of the heart monitor is important, emphasize it in this final scene) as she apologizes for everything then leaves. Dominic dies, "with a sorry on his lips." [END OF NOVEL]

I'm frozen to my chair except for my hand shaking the page. I can hear the sounds in my body. My heart beating, my blood rushing, my ear ringing. Then I feel everything at once, and I'm stomping towards Decker's room the next second.

Decker is lying in bed. Amelia is handing him some sleeping pills and a cup of water, but all I care about is that he's awake enough to listen.

"Decker, you've made a mistake," I tell him. I drop the outline on his nightstand.

Decker gives me an innocuous look. He's tired and about to take his meds and I'm interrupting his nightly routine, but I'm too angry to care.

"Care to elaborate?" he asks.

"Dominic dies, 'with a sorry on his lips'" I quote the outline. "What the hell is that?"

"Do you not like the phrasing?" he asks. "If you have a different wording choice, I'll hear it, but I'm very certain about that line—"

"That's not what I mean," I say. "I mean the whole scene. Why does Dominic Black have to die? Moreover, why does he have to die like *that*?"

"'Die like that'?"

"The way he does in the story! The greatest detective the city has ever seen, and he dies in some shitty hospital room, his wife leaves him, and nobody around him seems to care. How the hell does a man like Dominic Black go out like that?"

Decker's gaze softens and he lets out a sigh.

"Daniel," Decker says softly. He speaks like a parent calming a child. "I had the final line of this book in my head long before the first book was even written. Dominic was always meant to die. I knew from the beginning."

"But why?" I ask. "Even if you insist on killing him with the series, why does he...go out like that?"

Decker chuckles, and it takes all my willpower not to glare at him.

"You would've preferred he go out in a blaze of glory?" he says.

"I'd choose less cliché phrasing, but yes."

"Dominic Black is a selfish, self-destructive narcissist. He's a hero, yes, and he's saved a lot of people, but the man has more vices than teeth in his mouth. He drinks and shoots up every substance he can find, spits in the face of anyone who stands in his way, treats women like meat, and solves murders for his ego." Decker raises an eyebrow. "What about a man like that makes you think his death was going to be some grand, glorious event?"

"Because he's a hero to so many people!" I exclaim. "You write a guy who's a total badass only for him to die in a piss stain? You write dozens of books about this guy only to have him die alone in a shithole?"

"Daniel," Decker says. His voice sharpens. I can feel all the excitement I had this afternoon draining from me. "I always planned for Dominic Black to die, and to die in this manner. I said before I don't mind you adding your artistic license, but that is the one part of the outline I won't budge on. Add your own suggestions, make tweaks where you see fit. But Dominic's final chapter does not change."

He turns to Amelia, who hands him his pills and water. I watch him bring the little yellow pills to his wrinkled tongue, then swallow. He leans back and closes his eyes, and within seconds he starts to snore.

—

I spend the next two weeks writing in a haze. Despite my anger at Decker, the rage pushes me forward. I drink more caffeine than what's likely healthy. I board myself up in the guest room, and as I write, I can hear Decker's ragged breathing in the room down the hall.

The outline of the final novel is brilliant, as usual. Dominic Black finds himself trapped with a villain from his past who's been hovering over the whole series, still uncaught by the city's best detective. The one who represents all his demons. There are moments I get a thrill writing it, enough that I finish the first draft by the end of the third week.

Well, close to a first draft. I write up to chapter forty-seven and stop. My fingers hover over the keyboard. It's not writer's block. I know exactly what I'm supposed to write, and an idea of how to do it. But I can't bring myself to write those final words: "died with a sorry on his lips."

Dominic Black never said sorry. He did what he thought needed to be done, and he did it. He didn't break under people's scrutiny. He didn't apologize for any of his decisions if he thought they were the right ones. I don't know what madness has led Decker to think that this is how his detective should die. The old man must be senile or so hopped up on those meds Amelia gives him that he just forgot how to write his own protagonist.

I stare at the blinking cursor for hours. Then, I begin typing. I don't write what Decker put in the outline. My fingers will freeze up if I do. Instead, my mind starts to wander across the page. I rewrite the scene in a clean hospital room. His wife is by his side, holding his hand, saying she was wrong to doubt him and forgives him and promises to stay by his side forever. All his coworkers come to visit him. Reporters bang outside his door, begging to be let in, to see the city's hero after his daring mission. The kind of ending a hero like Dominic Black deserves.

I'm startled by a knock at the door. Amelia pokes her auburn head inside.

"Hey," she says. "How's the writing going?"

I glance at myself in a mirror on the wall. My hair's messy, I don't remember the last time I showered, and my eyes are baggy with too little sleep and too much caffeine to do anything about it.

"Coming along," I say. I move my things to the side and head into the connecting bathroom. I realize I've needed to piss for hours.

When I come back out, Amelia is looking at the laptop.

"Hey," I snap, then shut the laptop. "You shouldn't read something until it's finished."

"Sorry," she says. "I just wanted to take a little look. I'm curious how similar your writing style is to Decker's. If people will tell the difference or not."

I raise an eyebrow.

"You've read the series?"

"I only read the first couple of books," she says, then chuckles. "It's a long series. I'll get around to finishing it eventually." Then she gives me a look. "I read a bit of what you've written so far. I thought Decker's outline said Dominic dies in the end. Have you not gotten to that part yet?"

My neck grows hot.

"No, that…" My mind scrambles for an explanation. "That was just a writing exercise. I find it helps when creative block starts to creep in."

Amelia's not a writer, so she just nods. I wait for her to leave, but she continues to linger there. I open my laptop again, pull it onto my lap, and try to look busy.

"What do you think of the ending?" she asks.

I consider whether to give her the honest answer or not. I'm not sure why she wants to know, since she hasn't even read all the books.

"It's unexpected," I admit. "It takes balls to kill off your main character."

"Well, it is the end of the series. At least it leaves no mystery of what could happen to him next."

I respectfully disagree, but I don't bother to tell her that.

"Still," I say. "Unexpected and conclusive does not always mean satisfactory."

Amelia turns on her heels then heads into the hallway, closing the door behind her. I slump back in my seat and stare at what I've written. I was supposed to have a first draft done today, as per the publishing schedule. But every cell in my brain refuses to think of a way to make that shit ending work.

I think about all the fans, people like me who've always wondered how and when Dominic Black's story would end. I've read fan theories on forums, read articles and opinion pieces, talked with other readers. The idea of Dominic dying came up, but I never considered he'd die in the loser fashion Decker landed on.

Decker never wrote anything else besides the Dominic Black series. Aside from a few screenplays and anthology submissions, the series was his legacy. And I wasn't entirely sure if Decker really understood the legacy he was leaving with this ending. Fans may turn on him. Critics will tear apart the whole series because of one bad conclusion.

I look at the clock. It's nearly midnight. Amelia must have given Decker his pills, because his soft snores breathe through the walls. This literary giant is wasting away in his bed, totally oblivious to how his own readers might react to their hero dying in a dumpster.

Mitchell Decker is terminally ill. He doesn't have much longer to live. No one knows when exactly he'll go out, but it's any day now. His lungs might not wait for him to read the manuscript. He could be dead tomorrow, and no one would think twice about it.

He could be dead tomorrow, and no one would think twice about it.

—

Mitchell Decker is dying from lung cancer. Much like his protagonist, the man has spent decades smoking like a chimney. The problem is with his breathing. It's the breath in his chest that's killing him.

It's gotten worse. I stand over his bed and watch his chest shiver as it rises and falls, subtle enough that he looks corpse-still. You can barely hear his snores. You can barely hear anything in the house.

I'm quiet when I bring the pillow to his face. His body is weak, and Amelia's pills are still in their full effect. He only moves a little. In the seventh book in the series, *Dominic Black: City That Never Sleeps*, he investigates the death of a woman who died by being smothered with a pillow. He described her kicking and screaming and clawing at her unknown assailant. Decker's feeble body holds no such resistance. Within minutes, the subtle rise and fall of his chest goes still.

I shove the pillow back under his head. I peel off the plastic medical gloves I found with Amelia's stuff. I drop them off in a dumpster several miles from the house, at the very bottom of the trash heap.

The next morning, I seal the manuscript in a manila envelope and send it off.

—

Mitchell Decker is found dead the morning of October tenth. His death is sooner than expected and it takes no time for the media reports to point this out. The story plays out almost cinematically: Amelia wakes to go check on her employer, only to find he has stopped breathing. She rushes into the room of his "guest" downstairs, and he tearfully receives the news of the author's death.

Two weeks later, Decker's publisher announces the release date for his last novel completed just before his death. Months later, the book shoots to number one on every list. The readership consist of both devoted fans and those who read out of a sense of duty to the dead literary king. The fact that this is the last book of the series, and the news of Decker's death, help the sales skyrocket.

I decide to stay in Decker's house a little longer. He said I could stay as long as the story needed me to, and I'm not done just yet. I spend days turning over the book in my hand, rereading my favorite parts, rereading the ending. I look at reviews of the book online and see a division. The fans of the book love it, happy that Dominic's story concluded in a happy place. The other is critics, throwing around words like "character assassination" and "giving in to a Hollywood ending." I don't bother myself much with those. Critics will say anything to generate clicks, and at the end of the day, Dominic Black belongs to his fans, not people looking to make a few bucks.

I see Amelia a couple of times as she moves her things out of the house. I ask her if she read the book, and she says she did. She doesn't ask about the ending. I told her I had persuaded Decker to go with my ending before he died, and even she doesn't want to admit the story is better with my version.

—

Decker's funeral is at the same church in which he married his wife over sixty years ago. The service consists of his few remaining relatives and a bunch of his readers. I sit in the back row, watching weepy-eyed fans with their old signed copies. These people are just like me. People who've grown and evolved because of these books. I decide not to tell them the truth about Decker. Let them grieve.

The service goes as usual. The minister speaks over the coffin. Decker's remaining family offers a few eulogies. I let myself blend into the crowd of his readers, make them think I'm no different from them.

I think the service is about to end, but then the minister clears his throat.

"Before we leave today," he says. "We have one last speaker. Miss Amelia Rhodes was Decker's caretaker in the last days of his life in his at-home hospice care. She has asked to read something for us."

Amelia appears at the podium. Her beige uniform has been traded out for a black dress, and her auburn bun is now held together by a black beetle-shaped hair clip. She sets a slip of paper in front of her before she starts speaking.

"Thank you, father," she says. The microphone rings her static voice around the church. "I had the privilege of being with Decker in his final days. I didn't know him before my work with him, but we quickly became friends. I had been a fan of his books for years, and I was honored to be there for him in his last days. In the days leading up to his death, he asked me to read something at his service."

An overhead projector shows a written note on the wall above her. Amelia clears her throat to read. The note is simple and sweet. A series of thank you's to all his family and friends who've been there for him throughout his life, as well as a thank you to Amelia herself. It reads like an author's note at the end of a novel, which is fitting. I sit and listen patiently as she reads off the names of everyone Decker had to thank. Then she comes to the end.

"And finally, I want to thank Daniel Armstrong," she says.

My stomach spools out onto the floor. "Everyone in the audience looks confused, a few people across the room whisper "who?"

"Daniel is one of the most passionate, creative young minds I've met," Amelia continues. "I knew when I was unable to complete the last book in the series, I would need someone who cared for this series and its lead as much as I did. He finished the last book, and I can only hope I'll get a chance to read it before I pass. It's because of him you all can experience Dominic Black one final time."

Everyone in the room is looking around, whispering, talking, and some are starting to look at me.

"I remember the first night he came to stay with me, we had a great discussion about the book's ending. He was just as passionate as me about deciding how this series should end. Eventually, we came to the agreement that Dominic Black's death, while a choice not everyone will love, is the one that is best to conclude this troubled man's story."

"Death?"

The word whispers around the room. Now nearly half the room is looking at me and my shirt is leaking with sweat and there's red in my face. Amelia finishes reading the note, then turns her eyes straight to me.

"Daniel Armstrong is here with us tonight," she says. "And he's invited to speak for his hero if he'd like."

Everyone's looking at me, and the look in their eyes does indeed expect me to speak. I'm silent and shaking. I stand up from my seat, then rush in the other direction and leave.

There's a lot of mail arriving at Decker's house the following days. It's overflowing from the mailbox and clogging up my email. I sit on the guest room bed and dig through all of it. They're letters from fans. And critics. And Decker's family. All of them with different handwriting and different return addresses, but awash in a tidal wave of the same message: Who the hell am I, and what did I do to change the book.

The letters don't stop in the days following. At a certain point, I stop reading them and let them pile by the front door, letting them go straight to spam in my email. There's only so many times you can read the same inane questions without going crazy:

How are you?

Did you change Decker's ending?

You stole this book from him.

You're an imposter.

Go kill yourself.

Not all of them are negative. Some of them thank me for changing the ending, but even those ask why I went against Decker's request. It doesn't make any sense to me. I gave them what they wanted. None of us fans wanted Dominic Black to die, especially not the way Decker intended. I saved Dominic from the careless clutches of his creator, and all I get in return is hate mail from people I thought were true fans.

I'm startled by a knock at the door again, and by the same red-headed bun that started this whole thing.

"Sorry," Amelia says. "I forgot something when I was moving my things out, and just wanted to grab it real quick. Didn't mean to disturb you."

"Disruption accomplished," I say. I turn my squiggles chair to face her. "You wrote that eulogy, didn't you? I don't buy for a second that Decker wrote that and asked you to read it at the service."

Amelia purses her lips and looks at the floor.

"Daniel," she says. "After all this, you still can't believe that Decker means what he writes."

"He said to keep the ghostwriting part a secret," I say. "My name wouldn't be on the cover, but I'd get financial compensation."

"He did." Amelia raised her eyes back up to me. "But I disagreed with that premise. I saw how much this story meant to you, and I thought it was unfair you wouldn't be credited just to keep up some charade that he wrote the whole thing. I suggested to Decker that you get some kind of recognition for finishing the book. He agreed and decided to write one to read at the funeral." She purses her lips again. "I didn't make him do anything. I made a suggestion, and he agreed to it. I only went through with what he requested."

It takes all my willpower not to throw something at her.

"Of course," I say. My voice shakes. "You're just such a good person, aren't you? Just doing what you're told. Just going along with whatever the boss man says."

I drop my face into my hands. I can't even look at her or I'm going to do something I might regret.

"What're you working on?" she asks.

She's referring to my open laptop.

"I'm...working on the next book," I tell her. I lift my eyes to her. "I contacted the publisher, and they agreed that after the sales to renew the Dominic Black series for a few more books. Especially now that he's not dead. They made some arrangements and handed it over to me."

I wait for her response. There's something in her eyes I can't read. When she speaks, it's soft, like she's afraid her voice will break something.

"Decker..."

"Decker was wrong," I say. "He was some senile old man who forgot how to write his own character. Dominic Black is alive, and if Decker wants to crawl out of his grave to change that, he can come back into this house to stop me any time he wants."

I turn my chair back to face my computer. I can feel Amelia watching me from the door, like she thinks she can telepathically change my mind. "*I only read the first couple books*". No shit. No wonder she thought Decker's ending was good. She doesn't know shit about the series or Dominic Black.

I hear her footsteps and the roll of her suitcase down the hall. Minutes later, the front door opens and shuts. The house is hollow and empty. The quiet is eerie and serene. It's the perfect place for a writer to focus.

I open a new document and write the first line:

The first thing on Dominic Black's mind as he left Montefiore Medical Center was the taste of blood in his mouth...

Animal Eyes

Papa and Uncle Teddy were going at it. It was one in the morning, and I hadn't even fallen asleep when I heard them downstairs. I could recognize each of them by the noises they made, the sounds of their footsteps. My dad wore boots with a slight heel that tapped against the wooden floorboards. Uncle Teddy wore Nikes that squeaked. I could hear them both pacing around the kitchen.

"I ain't even seen her in weeks!" Uncle Teddy shouted.

"You came over during Christmas," Papa replied. "You kept going on about how great her stuffing was."

"What'd you want me to say? That her cooking tasted like shit?"

They must have been talking about Mama. Mama left to visit a friend's house a couple of days ago, and none of us had seen her since. Based on the commotion downstairs, Papa was certain Uncle

Teddy had something to do with it. He was the last person to have seen her besides us, and Papa was convinced that he was the "friend" Mama went to visit.

The shouting had only gotten louder downstairs. Paper threw out more accusations and Uncle Teddy threw out more defenses. I'd gotten used to our house being a loud place at night. Even when Mama was here, Papa would still find something to make noise about. In the seventeen years I'd lived under this roof, I taught myself the art of falling asleep without silence to soothe me.

"Jacob?" Toby's voice peeped at my side. I lifted my head from my pillow. My little brother was six years old and had been wearing the same Batman pajamas ever since Mama left, since Papa didn't know how to use the washing machine. Mama tried to teach him, but he just got mad and accused her of calling him stupid. So my brother stood beside my bed in his stinky, food-stained pajamas with his stuffed elephant in his arm.

"Toby?" I said.

I watched him twist the stuffed elephant's trunk with his hand. He always did that when he was scared.

"Can I sleep with you tonight?"

This was not the first time Toby asked to sleep in my bed. While I could sleep through just about anything, Toby was not so restful. Tonight was, without a doubt, one of the loudest nights to sleep through.

Papa shouted so loud the walls shook. The noise was followed by the clink of glasses across the kitchen table. Toby covered his ears and squeezed his eyes shut.

"Come here," I told him.

I scooted my back against the wall and made room in the one-person bed for Toby to lay down beside me. His clothes smelled like shit, but the noise downstairs wasn't getting any quieter.

Toby was a surprise. Mama and Papa had expected me, but they hadn't planned on having more kids after me. When Toby came along, Aunt Grace and I were the first people to see him. I looked down at Toby's pudgy little face wrapped in a blue cotton blanket. He made a little squeak when he sneezed. It didn't take me long to figure out that he belonged to me as much as to Mama and Papa. Maybe even more so as the years went on.

"Where else would she be?" Papa yelled. "Every time you're here you two are all over each other. I'm surprised a pussy like you even had the stones to come back here."

"I came here cause you asked," Uncle Teddy said. "If you want me to leave so bad, then I'll go."

"I never said we were done!"

The kitchen erupted into noises. Grunts, curses, furniture scratching across the floor, and a glass cup cracking on the floor. Toby stiffened beside me, and I put an arm over him. Papa got mad, but this felt different.

All the cacophony downstairs ended with the backdoor slamming so loud the walls visibly shook. Toby made a sound and buried his head in my chest. I went completely still and listened to the two men's voices outside.

I tried to make out what they were saying. Me and Toby's room sat upstairs on the side of the house closest to the backyard, and I could hear them down on the ground below us. I was certain they were about to start fighting. Papa was always picking fights with Uncle Teddy, and this wouldn't be the first or last time he left our house with a couple of bruises.

I heard their shoes squelching the wet mud outside. Their voices were spread with dirt, and I could hear the rustle of their jeans and jackets as they struggled against each other. I held Toby close and closed my eyes. By morning, this would be over.

Then came a sound that shot me right out of my skin. Toby heard it too and started quietly weeping. I could feel his eyes wetting my t-shirt.

"What's happening, Jacob?" he whispered.

I listened closely outside. The sound had been a loud, white-hot pop. My stomach filled with cold water. I recognized that sound. It was a sound I always subconsciously expected to hear after one of Papa's outbursts, but it had been so long since I heard it that I didn't recognize it at first.

I moved to crawl out of bed. Toby grabbed the fabric of my shirt and tried to pull me back down.

"I don't want to be alone," he said.

My brother's cheeks were shiny wet in the moonlight tumbling out our window. I closed my hand over his.

"I'm not going anywhere," I told him. "I'm just gonna peek out the window."

"What if he sees you?"

"I'll make sure he won't."

And to make sure of it, I kneeled to the floor and army-crawled to the window facing the backyard. I lifted my eyes just enough to see over the window ledge. The land beyond our backyard was trees that separated our neighborhood from the next. Amber street lights in the next neighborhood blinked through the trees to create spots of light between the branches. The lights and full moon made just enough light that I could see my dad's silhouette moving towards the woods. He was hunched down, walking at a slow pace. His hands reached down to something near the ground. Uncle Teddy was nowhere.

A naive part of me wondered if Uncle Teddy had just left. Papa got out his pistol and fired a round into the sky just to scare him off. But as my eyes adjusted to the dark, I could see a long stretch of slick mud that ran the ground from our backyard towards Papa's direction. Right by Papa's hand, I could see a flash of red like Uncle Teddy's Red Sox baseball cap.

"What's there?" Toby whispered.

It took me minutes to respond. I didn't blink or move as I watched Papa drag our uncle deeper into the trees to do God knows what with him. When Papa's silhouette disappeared, that's when I shut the window blinds and sunk to the floor.

"Jacob?" Toby asked. "What happened?"

My body went from still and empty to buzzing a million things. My head became a wasps' nest of thoughts and pumping blood and a scream in my skin. Uncle Teddy was dead, and Papa had shot him.

Papa was no stranger to aggression, but his anger never hit anyone directly. There was something inside him that wanted to hurt, to stir fear. I imagined it'd been this way most of his life. He'd been born in this town and had little prospect for dying out of it. He threw things, he broke things, he yelled at people. But he never lay a hand on us, a fact he always brought up whenever anyone dared to challenge him. I bet he'd say the same thing about Uncle Teddy. *What? I didn't lay a finger on him* he'd say while smoke poured from his pistol. I chuckled a little at the thought. I was delirious.

"What's so funny, Jacob?"

Toby's voice finally reached me, and I looked up at him. My little brother had stopped crying, but his dark eyes still shimmered. A tuft of the dark hair we shared fell over his eye. I imagined Mama smoothing it out of the way.

But Mama wasn't here anymore. This meant the only person left to keep my brother safe was me. I could handle just about anything Papa threw at me. I could duck away, keep a straight face while he yelled. But I made a promise when Toby was born that Papa would never hurt him, and I'll be damned if he did today.

I made the decision so fast that I was on my feet before it finished crossing my mind. I pulled a pair of jeans out of our shared dresser and over my boxers. Then I slid on my jacket and started searching around for a pair of dry socks.

"What's going on, Jacob?" Toby asked. His voice was getting impatient. "Tell me what happened."

I found a pair of socks, fumbled them on in the dark then shoved my feet into my sneakers. I had too many thoughts in my head to think of a proper way to explain to Toby what happened. I tried to calculate how far Papa had gotten into the woods, and how long it would take for him to dispose of Uncle Teddy, depending on whether he was burying him or dumping him into the river. And how long it would take for him to come back.

I thought of calling the police, but our phone downstairs hadn't been working since yesterday and my parents couldn't afford to buy me a cellphone. And even if the phone did work, I didn't know what Papa would do when he got back, and I didn't trust the cops to get here in time before he did.

"I...I'll tell you later, Toby," I told him. I found his Superman jacket under his bed. "You and I need to leave right now."

"Why?" he asked as I ushered him out of bed. "Where are we going?"

"Aunt Grace's house," I said.

Aunt Grace was about the only safe place I could think for us to go. While Dad brought Uncle Teddy into the family, Mama brought Aunt Grace. Unlike Mama, whose philosophy was that fighting Papa only made matters worse, Aunt Grace was never afraid to call Papa out on his shit and didn't even flinch when he threw a frying pan at her once. She always made me promise after we visited her that I would call her in case of an emergency. And right now, I needed to get Toby somewhere safe. Somewhere with a working phone.

I placed the jacket over Toby's shoulders and tried to help him into his socks and shoes. But he wasn't being very cooperative. My baby brother kept asking me over and over again, and I kept telling him I'd tell him later, then he started yelling until I finally snapped.

"Papa's angry," I growled at him. "And if you don't shut your lip, he'll be even angrier, and it'll be on both our asses!"

That made him go quiet. My brother's eyes went shiny, and his lip quivered. I wanted to kick myself. One of the downsides of always shielding my brother from Papa is that he never fully understood the extent of Papa's threats. I hated yelling at him, but I needed him to understand that asking questions was a privilege for those whose survival wasn't a concern.

"I'm sorry," I told him. I wiped a tear from his cheek with my thumb. "I didn't mean to yell. I promise, promise, promise I'll tell you when we get to Aunt Grace's house, okay?"

His lip still quivered, but he nodded and remained quiet. I wanted to comfort him more, but then I remembered how long it'd been since Papa went out into the woods. I peeked through the crack in the blinds. Papa hadn't come back yet, but I could see his figure in the trees, and he wasn't dragging anyone behind him this time.

"We gotta go," I told Toby. I grabbed his wrist and hurried him downstairs. He was slow on his little legs, but he kept up as we fumbled down. My eyes scattered the place for the car keys. I could feel every second melting past us, each one another foot closer that Papa got to the house. In the kitchen, I found shattered glass on the floor, and I had to usher Toby away so he wouldn't step on any of the shards. I side-stepped the mess and found the car keys in the bowl on the kitchen counter.

I heard steps approaching the back of the house. I clutched the keys in my fist and scooped Toby up in my arms. I rushed out the front door, not even bothering to shut it, and rushed down to Papa's truck. I heard the back door open and Papa's footsteps stumble in.

"Get in and stay quiet," I whispered to Toby.

I helped him into the passenger seat and strapped on his seatbelt. As I rounded to the other side and opened the driver's side door, I heard what was unmistakably Papa's voice howling from inside.

"What the hell are you two doing?" he called.

My heart suspended in my chest while I slid into the driver's seat, slammed the door shut, and locked it. I didn't even bother to put on my seatbelt before I shoved the key into the ignition.

The engine rumbled to life, and as the headlights blinked on, they landed on Papa standing in the driveway. His eyes glowed round and bright red in the headlights. For a split second, the image of running him over crossed my mind, sending his blood and brains across the white garage door. But then I heard Toby scream next to me, and I backed out of the driveway and onto the road before Papa could round to my side.

Thank God the neighborhood was empty, because if anyone had been standing on our street that night, I would have run them over as I stomped on the gas. The old truck groaned down the road, and I didn't stop until long after I couldn't hear Papa's raging expletives anymore.

—

The drive to Aunt Grace's house wasn't that long. She lived on a different side of town than us, in a nicer neighborhood where people didn't make as much noise at night. But the minutes that stretched between our house and Aunt Grace's felt like days. My eyes were red and crusty while I watched the headlights gobble up the white lines that dotted the center of the road. Toby remained quiet beside me. He'd been shaking before, but now I think he may have fallen asleep. I didn't bother to look over and check. I didn't dare tear my eyes from the road.

Every other pair of headlights sent a spike of fear in me. It was almost five a.m. There was no reason for anyone else to be out this late. It wasn't until we were stopped at a red light, no cars passing by, that a realization dropped into my stomach. Uncle Teddy's car was still parked in front of our house, and I had no doubts that Papa would've found his keys.

I looked up in the rearview mirror. The road behind us was pitch black, no other cars following us. My mind began to spiral with everything that could go to shit. What if Papa figured out we were going to Aunt Grace's, and he was already there waiting for us?

What if he tried to hurt Aunt Grace, too?

I heard Toby breathing softly beside me. I guess he had fallen asleep after all, the stuffed elephant still tucked faithfully in his elbow. I tried to push all the bad thoughts from my mind. Something I'd gotten good at. I would deal with whatever came next when we got to Aunt Grace's.

After forty-five minutes that felt like forty-five hours, my headlights met the red bricks of our aunt's house. I didn't want to announce to anyone watching that we were here, so I parked the car a few yards down from her house. I woke Toby up and guided him through the dark towards the house.

I knocked at the front door. It was late, and she was likely asleep. I kept knocking just loud enough that she'd hear, but not so much to alert anyone nearby. I kept knocking for ten minutes, and nothing. I rang the doorbell. I cringed at the loud ding that echoed through the house. I tried it twice. Thrice. Nothing.

"Is she still sleeping?" Toby asked.

My heartbeat was getting loud in my ears. My teeth gritted together, and I was shaking. There was no car in the driveway. I went around to the side door that led into the garage. It was almost impossible to see through the pitch black in the door window, but I couldn't see any outline of a car. I checked through the front window. The top floor window that led into the bedroom was dark.

"Fuck," I growled.

Toby grabbed onto my hand harder. Aunt Grace wasn't home. Maybe she was wherever Mama was, or just out of town. I wanted to take the flower pot by her front door and smash it onto the concrete.

She promised I thought. *She promised we could come to her if we needed help, and she's not even here.*

But I didn't have time to stew in my anger for long. Toby tugged at my hand, and I glanced up in time to see a pair of headlights turn into the neighborhood. My chest went cold when I recognized the green paint job of Uncle Teddy's car.

I grabbed Toby and raced us around to the back of the house. My eyes darted around for someplace to hide. Then my eyes crossed the field to a barn house belonging to one of the neighbors. I heard Uncle Teddy's car park in the driveway. There wasn't any more time to weigh options.

I scooped up Toby again in my arms, and I darted across the field with more fury than I ever had before. The full moon beamed down on us like it wanted us to get caught. We were out in the open of the field, no trees or bushes to hide us. If Papa came around the house and looked, he'd see me running.

I didn't look behind me until we made it to the barn. I glanced back and saw Papa at the back of the house, his back to us while he trailed a flashlight over some bushes. I let out a sigh when I saw the barn wasn't locked and the door creaked open. The place smelled of bile and feces, but it was dark and safe.

"Let's stay in here," I told Toby.

I looked at Toby, and he stood back away from me, his body frozen to where he was standing.

"Toby, get in."

"It's too dark in there...and I'm scared of the horses."

I resisted the urge to roll my eyes. Toby had a phobia of barn animals ever since he got bit by a neighbor's horse when we visited their pen. Despite us living out in a rural farm town, he never got close to animals. But my head was too full of more pressing dangers to remember.

"They're in their pens, they won't hurt you," I told him. "And I'm right here, nothing in the dark will get you."

But Toby shook his head and wouldn't budge. My pulse was starting to ricochet. I looked back up at the house. Papa was facing our direction now with his flashlight on the field. He could see us at any moment.

"Now's not the time to be scared, Toby," I told him. "Get in."

"I don't wanna," Toby backed away from the door. "Can we hide behind it instead?"

My stomach was starting to boil. Toby had no idea what was about to happen if he didn't hurry. He had no idea it was *my ass* that was getting worse if we got caught. I was doing this all for him. And he was being a scared little turd.

"We don't have time for that, Toby," I growled. "Now get in there before I hurt you."

Toby's eyes went wide, but this time I was too pissed to feel sorry. I grabbed him by the arm and started yanking him in. He dug his heels in the dirt trying to pull away.

"It's too dark!" Toby cried. The sound was loud enough that Papa could hear it. I kept glancing across the field waiting to see him charging at us.

"Hey, who's out there!"

I looked up and saw the lights in the neighboring house flick on. A silhouette appeared out the window. The neighbor heard us and was probably wondering about all the noise happening around his barn.

I turned to my brother and shoved him through the door. He stumbled face-first into the dirt while I shut the door behind us, leaving it in near pitch black.

All the barn animals looked our way. Cows, chickens, two horses, all of them started to stir at their new guests. But over all the noise I could hear Toby sniffling. I dropped to my knees and fumbled around the ground for him. When I felt my hand touch his leg, he immediately pulled it away.

"Don't touch me," he spat. "I'm…"

I squinted in the dark. A beam of moonlight from between the boarded walls streaked into the barn, and over my brother's arm. A streak of red ran down from his elbow, right where some rock on the ground had cut him when he fell.

For several seconds, I forgot all about Papa and the neighbor, both of whom no doubt were on their way. But I stared at the bleed-ing red line on my brother's arm, and all the anger drained away to leave my body cold. I did that. I'd never done that to my brother before. Hell, not even Papa had ever made Toby bleed before.

Toby scooted away from me until he was against a wall in the corner. I stumbled through the dark until I found a pile of hay in the corner next to a goat pen.

"Get in there," I told Toby. "And stay quiet."

The two of us bundled into the hay. We shoveled handfuls of it all over us until we couldn't see the outside. The stuff itched like hell and was infested with bugs. I could see Toby trying to hold in a sneeze. I covered his mouth and nose with my hand.

I don't know how long we were in that hayloft. The small pocket of air we waited in became thick with sweat and bugs. Toby dripped with perspiration, making his pajamas only stink more. I wanted to rage at someone. He was shaking in my arms, his hand still pressed to the wet cut I put on him. I wanted to rage at Mama for disap-pearing out of nowhere, without taking us with her or even offer a hint about where she'd gone. For giving Papa a reason to chew out Uncle Teddy and leading to this whole shitty night in the place. I wanted to rage at Aunt Grace for not keeping her promise to be there for us. I wanted to rage at Uncle Teddy for testing my father until he finally blew up. A part of me even wanted to rage at Toby. Doing this alone was enough, but now I was responsible for some-one else too.

Instead, I turned my quiet ire onto the other living things around me. The animals in the barn kept making noise. I thought they would simply simmer down after the initial shock of our ar-rival. But the damn cows and horses didn't stop groaning and the damn chickens didn't stop clucking and the damn goats didn't stop bleating.

Then in the cacophony, another sound came. A pair of foot-steps just outside the barn, right behind the wall that Toby and I crammed against. A light beamed through the cracks in the boards of the wall.

"I know you're around here, boys," Papa growled in the dark. His voice was still hot and angry, the rush of a kill was still frying in his heart. "I've got all night, so you boys might as well step out."

I pressed my hand tight against Toby's mouth. I could feel his tears, snot, and drool wetting my hand, which was already slick with sweat. But I clenched my jaw shut and I covered up his.

The goat in the pen next to us pressed his head in our direction and made a loud bleat. I wanted to shoot its little head off and throw it by its horns. The footsteps moved away from us, and for a second, I thought he was leaving. I thought maybe we could make a run for it, take off into the woods, bang on the neighbors' doors, and scream out our lungs until someone woke up long enough to help us.

And then I heard a creak as the barn doors opened, and I caught a flash of light trail itself around the barn. I peeked through a small opening in the hay pile. I watched a small spotlight glide over the pens as the animals sprung to life. As the light passed over each of them, I got a good look at the animals. The cows, the horses, the chickens, the goats. The light turned all their eyes round and red.

And they were all looking at us.

"Who's in here?" a voice said.

The voice made me pause for a moment. It didn't sound like Papa's. It didn't sound angry. It sounded concerned, and I wondered for a moment if it was the owner of the barn, if he finally came out to check the ruckus happening outside his house. He'd woken up. He'd see Papa and chase him off the property. Maybe he'd help us. Maybe he'd get a bandage for Toby's arm...

But then again, maybe it was Papa, and this was just a trick to get us to expose ourselves. I was tired and delirious. I was wondering if I was hearing things wrong. The footsteps grew closer, and I could feel the heat from the flashlight.

The footsteps stopped right in front of the hay pile.

"Come on out," the voice said again.

I couldn't tell if it was Papa's voice. I lowered my eyes to Toby, shaking and quietly weeping in my arms. My fear and anger curdled like milk in my chest. Toby was small, even for a six-year-old. He'd always been that way, and probably always would.

I knew he always would. Because I knew there would be a *would*. I would assure Toby that *he will*. My hands felt around until I touched the blood pouring from my brother's arm. Blood poured because of me. Some part of me had slipped away and left only my papa in my place. I wasn't going to let that happen again. My baby brother was going to walk out of this barn, and whoever held that flashlight was not going to do a damn thing to stop it.

I moved my brother behind me and rose to my feet. Bits of hay fell from my clothes onto the ground. The light beamed into my eyes. I couldn't tell what I looked like to whoever was on the other end of that flashlight. I imagined my eyes like an animal's: red, round, and glowing.

When You Come Home

I don't remember when I started calling you Mimi. According to my mother, it started with how I always used to greet you when I was little. Whenever I saw you, I would stick my arms out and yell, "Me! Me!" as a command for you to pick me up. I always greeted you that way, and eventually, that greeting turned into the nickname I called you ever since.

When I show up at your house, I glance down at a spot on the floor where the morning sun streaks onto the wooden boards. For a moment, I consider taking a seat on the floor and waiting for you there. I could sit there with my legs crossed, and when you walk through the door, I'll be there, and I'll lift my arms and say "Me! Me!" like I'm four again. The thought makes me chuckle.

The door shuts behind me. Your house hasn't changed a bit since you left. It's the same house Grandpa bought the night before your wedding. The wooden door makes that same slamming sound as it did when he carried you through the front in your lacy white dress. I glance at the picture of you two across the room. The photo has yellowed like a neglected tooth, with little crinkles and the frame covered in a thin membrane of dust.

Then I think: I should probably wipe that.

I know you well, Mimi, and I know the thing you love second to your friends and family is cleanliness. Even with the time you've been out, the house has remained mostly clean. But still, I know the last thing you'll want to see after weeks in the hospital is a dusty house.

I start with all the flat surfaces. I still remember where you keep all the cleaning supplies, under the kitchen sink with the same yellow rubber gloves. I slip them on. You must have cleaned before you left because they still feel warm from your fingers.

I squeeze one hand into a fist; then I use the other to grab the Clorox. I wipe down every flat surface I can find. The dining room table, careful to scrub extra by the end seat where Grandpa always sat at Thanksgiving. The green kitchen counter where I always insisted on sitting, where I sniffed at your lemon cookies in the oven. I swear I can smell a lifetime of meals as I move from one surface to the next.

In the living room, I hear my phone buzz from my handbag on the coffee table. It's probably Mom. Always a worrier bee, as you used to call her. You'd whisper that to me conspiratorially when she wasn't around. It always used to amaze me how someone as carefree as you could create someone as neurotic as my mom. I guess sometimes the apple does fall far from the tree.

Mom doesn't know I came back to your house, but I want to make sure the place is in shape before you come home. The phone stops buzzing by the time I put the Clorox and rubber gloves back right where they were before in the cabinet under the kitchen sink. As I stand up, I notice the bowl of fruit at the end of the counter. There's a couple of lemons left, and an idea creeps into my head.

I grab a few from the bowl, then search the cabinets until I find the family recipe book. When I pull it from the upper cabinet, it's brittle in my hands. The pages have yellowed, corners creased and folded from years of use. Inside the pages are filled with your blue, swirling cursive. I run my fingers along the ink embedded into paper, then get to work finding all the ingredients. A clean house and sweets to come home to. You've got yourself a pretty damn good granddaughter, Mimi.

Salt, flour, butter, lemon juice, eggs, I barely even open the recipe book as I grab all the ingredients. I list them off in my head one by one. Everything sticks together into a creamy, buttery goop. I grab a spoon out of the drawer and start scooping yellow blobs onto a metal tray.

"Enough to fill a spoon," I repeat.

While the cookies bake, I pace around the place. You always used to tease me about how I always walk on my tiptoes, and I would respond with something amusing like, "I'm practicing for when I wear high heels as an adult."

I walk along the hall and upstairs. The wooden boards creak under my steps. It barely feels like any time has passed since you left because the whole place smells like you. The hallways smell like the hairspray you've worn religiously since the sixties; the carpet is still lined with a sprinkle of fur from our old family husky. And at the end of the hall behind the wooden door with the silver knob is your room.

The first things I see when I open the door are a pile of clothes scattered around the bed, and a box on the ground. Your closet door is open and empty, and I stop for a moment and cock my head in confusion. Then I realize Mom must have come here earlier. Maybe that's why she didn't want me coming over. She wants to reorganize your stuff because God forbid she does not slather her neurosis all over everything.

I kick the box into the corner and start putting all your clothes back. Your church dresses arranged neatly in the closet, followed by your old nightgowns that still smell like baby powder, then your teddy bear shirts. I take the rest of your clothes and fold them one by one. "Sleeves in like a hug" I chuckle as I drop a blue sweater into the drawers. Mom emptied those, too.

As I finish folding the last stack of sweaters, I open the bottom drawer and freeze. A turquoise circle nestles in the drawer, almost like it was hidden. I pull it out, examine the yellow label in the center: EYES ON THE CLOUDS/STANLEY WESTBROOK.

That name rings like a song in my ears. Stanley Westbrook was an obscure blues artist from the sixties, who you dated before meeting Grandpa. He only produced one record, the first of which he'd given to you, and you kept ever since. You never told Grandpa you knew Westbrook, but it was one of the many secrets we kept between us. I run my fingers around the record. My fingers check for scratches, feel for the place your hands touched it, like our thumb-prints overlapping. The songs start spilling from some deep recession in my brain, each one bringing me back to church communions, running down toy store aisles, biting into funnel cake at the fall fair.

Downstairs, I hear the oven ding. I tuck the record under my arm and carry it downstairs. I set it on the table while I pull the metal pan out. The second I open the oven door, the smell is over-whelming. It engulfs me in a puff of nostalgia until I swear I can feel you beside me like a phantom limb.

I set the cookies on top of the oven, grab the Westbrook record off the table, then take it into the living room. My eyes immediately move to the corner for the turntable, but in the corner, all I see is a box with a photo frame and a vase inside. Goddammit, Mom, stay out of Mimi's stuff.

I walk over and dig until I find it at the bottom. I pull it out, set it on the table in the corner, and start setting it up. The turntable is a pale, eggshell blue. A gift from Grandpa on your first anniversary. And just like the cookie recipe, I don't need help sliding the record into place and sending it spinning. Westbrook's voice balloons into the air, and I sway my hips a little.

With the lemon cookies sufficiently cooled, I stack them neatly onto a blue plate then take them out to the living room. The record makes a soft popping sound when it switches tracks. I take one of the cookies off the plate and bring it to my lips, using my teeth to break off a piece. The tarty, lemony sweetness spreads across my tongue. I think for a second, I should wait for you to get here first, but given your sweet tooth, I bet the sooner-rather-than-later approach to cookies is something you'd agree with.

The white light streaming through the window starts to dim to gold. I finish the cookie, wiping the crumbs from my fingers and shirt. I realize it too late before they fall onto the carpet.

"Dammit," I say. "Guess it's time for the vacuum again."

Just as I stand up to grab the vacuum from the closet, my phone rings again. I swipe it up before I can check the caller ID, expecting to hear you chirping from the end. As if you knew I was having sweets without you, and you had to rectify the situation.

"Sarah?"

My smile droops.

"Mom," I say.

"Honey, where are you?"

"At Mimi's house."

I hear her sigh on the other end, and I roll my eyes.

"Why are you there?" she asks.

"I thought I'd clean the place up. I made some cookies, too. The lemon ones she always made on Easter." There's a pop in the corner. The track changes again, this time the song is a loud crescendo, one that fills the room like smoke.

"What's that noise, Sarah?" Mom asks.

"I found the old Stanley Westbrook album. Do you remember it? Mimi always put this on while we baked together. The one with the song about swimming in the creek?"

Mom's voice is so soft I almost don't hear it.

"Yeah, I remember it," she says.

I reach down and grab another cookie off the plate.

"I swear, I thought I'd forgotten all the words, but it's all coming back. It's like...I dunno, muscle memory for song lyrics or something." I take a bite and try to sing the lines through a mouthful of lemony sugar. "*Take me to the creek...sink me in the summer moon...*"

I move around the room. I swing my hips and swerve my shoulders as Westbrook's voice caresses the walls. On the phone, I hear Mom make a sound, something like she's about to sneeze, except it sounds like something in her throat. I smile. She's trying not to laugh. Beneath all the despondency she's kept up since you've been away from the house, she can't help but laugh when she hears that record. I hear her sniffle.

"Sarah," she chokes. "How long are you planning to stay there?"

"Just until Mimi gets home. I told you, I cleaned up everything for her, made her a snack." My voice sharpens a little. "I put back all the stuff you tried to box away."

"Because I knew you'd try to keep all her things. You don't...you won't understand that she doesn't need any of that anymore."

I chuckle.

"Yeah," I say sarcastically. "What kind of grandma doesn't need her clothes and stuff?"

Mom is silent.

"One who isn't going back inside that house again."

I roll my eyes again. Classic Mom, trying to catastrophize everything. A few days in the hospital, and suddenly Mom thinks you've moved to some distant country or something. I can already hear you laughing over the ridiculousness of this conversation.

"Bye, Mom," I say, then hang up.

Westbrook's voice carries its way across the room, and by the time the golden light outside turns blue, the plate only has one cookie left. I feel so bloated. I used to feel that way after you and I gorged on these cookies.

"That's just your happy stuffing," you said, then gave my belly a poke. "Stuffed like a Thanksgiving turkey."

I stand in the middle of the living room and sway to the last verse of the record. For a second, I wonder what you'd think if you saw me standing here. Nineteen years old, too big to sit on the counter, but I can still remember how to make lemon cookies and turn on a Westbrook album on the turntable.

I guess I'll just have to wait until you come home.

A Song Named "Ruby"

There's a song stuck in my head. It's been that way for months now. It doesn't help that it's been playing endlessly on the radio. It's been crawling up every music chart. You can't change to any radio station that isn't playing it on what feels like an infinite loop. It's enough to drive you insane. Which is appropriate since insanity is my intention.

The taxi meets me at the edge of the block. I step out of the rain and into the backseat. My feet are freezing and sore. These stilettos were not made for standing out on a wet concrete sidewalk. I wonder how hookers do it.

"Where to?" the driver asks.

I shut the side door.

"The New Yorker Hotel," I say.

The taxi pulls down the street. The rain is hard enough now that it creates a misty wall steaming over the skyscrapers. The driver keeps eyeing me through the rearview mirror.

His hand moves down to the radio and turns the volume up.

"You heard this song?" he asks.

I'm not in the mood for small talk, but giving someone what they want is usually the quickest way to get them to shut up.

"Yeah," I say.

"It's real good," he says. "I heard somewhere that the band is in town. They just played at the Apollo Theater." He pauses and looks at me in the rearview again. "I think they're staying at the New Yorker. Maybe you'll get to be the lucky lady who runs into them."

I purse my lips and look out the window. The driver seems to take the hint and turns his eyes back onto the road. But the song keeps playing on the radio. Its lyrics have scratched themselves into my brain, but they still sting to hear.

Ruby, Ruby red
Gone and lost her pretty head
Hear her down, down below
Hear her reap what I have sown

———

Two years ago, a news story trickled from the local stations of Wisconsin to the national airwaves. It spent a decent amount of time in the limelight despite the complete unoriginality of the story. Another young woman had been abducted and barely escaped with her life. The story was no doubt followed closely by discussions between parents and their daughters. Fathers buying their daughters pepper spray and mothers showing them how to hold their keys between their fingers.

I had those same cautionary tales told to me throughout the first eighteen years of my life. I was told to avoid going to second locations with people I didn't know, stay close to a group, and don't do anything provocative. Warnings that I should try not to be like *those* girls. The ones who made stupid decisions and got themselves killed. And I was good at it for a long time. I was a nice girl, and bad things don't happen to nice girls.

I continued to be a nice girl no matter what I did. At home with my parents, at school with my teachers, and on the weekends when I went to my friends' houses. The last night I saw them was the day before graduation. The air was getting sticky, and my friend's brother had a vintage record player he wanted to show us.

I sat on the couch in my friend's basement, a red solo cup of fruit punch in my hand while my friends cracked open Budweiser's from the mini-fridge in the corner. Beside me was my friend, her brother, and two older coworkers of his from down at their dad's mechanic shop. I was wearing a new denim skirt and a band-tee I found at the thrift store.

While my friend's brother attempted to get the old, popping record player to work, my friend talked to the two coworkers. It was hard to gauge their ages. Older than us by a lot, but no grey in their hair. I had seen the two of them over at my friend's house often. They seemed cool, and never bailed on us if we slipped a few beers. One of them was a lot chattier than the other, and he and my friend carried most of the conversation. The other guy just smiled and sipped tentatively at his drink. I didn't blame him. I wasn't much of a talker either. I never really knew what to say most of the time, hence why my friends were the ones who had to drag me to social gatherings.

My friend's brother managed to get the player to work, and the opening chords sputtered into the room.. The record popped a couple of times before the song fully kicked in. I recognized the band as Sublime, but I couldn't quite remember the name of the song. Most of the music I listened to back then needed to be kept discreet from my parents, so titles sometimes escaped me. The album cover lay on the table: The image of a frowning sun, the title "40oz to Freedom" scrawled across the bottom.

The whole group started singing along with the track. I only half-remembered the lyrics, so I just fumbled along until we came to the words I remembered:

"They locked him up and threw away the key...Well, I can't take pity on men of his kind..."

The quiet guy noticed my bad lip-syncing, and he gave me a grin and shook his head. Looks like both of us were rock novices. Around the time the album sputtered to an end, my friend was lying on the floor rubbing her belly and her brother's hand was shaking to change the record player. I decided then to head home. If I left then, I could get home before my parents freaked out about missing curfew.

I left the basement and walked out the front door. It took me only a second to realize I wasn't alone. One of the coworkers, the quiet one who disappeared a few minutes before me, was standing over his car with the hood open. He snapped his head over his shoulder like I'd startled him.

"Sorry," I said. "Just leaving."

His face softened, and he smiled. The only light on the street came from the house behind us, but I could still see his face. Perfect white teeth.

"No problem," he said.

I made my way to my car parked next to his, but I stopped to watch him fiddle with the mechanical guts under the hood. I didn't know anything about cars, but I liked watching him work. I kept trying to remember if I ever caught his name. Something with a J...

"Hey," he said.

His voice stopped me, and I turned on my heels.

"I'm so sorry," he said. "Could you grab something from the back of the trunk for me real quick? I can't take my hand off the gauge or it'll break, could you grab the wrench with the blue handle in the trunk? It should be unlocked."

I was a nice girl, so of course, I helped him.

I rounded the back to the trunk of the car. Through the living room curtains, I could see the silhouettes of the others fumbling upstairs. I opened the trunk and leaned inside. I found the toolbox and started digging for the wrench.

"What did you say it looked like again?" I asked.

I heard him coming around the side to show me. Then I remembered: He couldn't take his hand off the thing, right?

The question only had a second to cross my mind, because my head hit the carpeted inside of the trunk, and the door was shut and locked before my friends in the living room could hear the scream from my throat.

———

I don't remember much in the eight months that followed. My therapist says it's a trauma response. The memories are too painful, so my brain lets them slip. I don't remember my nineteenth birthday, and not just because it's easy to lose track of time when you're kept somewhere where you can't see the sun rise and fall. I can recall the moment a guy in a SWAT uniform took my hand in his glove and pulled me out of the ground into the sun, how hot it was after not seeing it in so long. I can't remember what I must have looked like in the mirror that day, but that's not exactly a memory I think needs to be saved.

Not that that girl from the ground was never documented. When my parents weren't locking me in the house to prevent more perfect-teeth strangers from snatching me up, they were locking me away from the endless parade of people with cameras. Reporters who wanted stories, publishers with book deals, true-crime podcasters who wanted interviews, Hollywood types thirsty for their next hit docu-series. All of them came for Ruby Dowell like gentlemen callers. My parents refused them all and wouldn't let me speak to any of them. And while they tried to hide it, I could sense what was happening in the outside world: I had just finished high school, and already the world had decided for me who I was: Ruby Dowell, the girl from the papers. The girl who was kept underground.

Most people didn't remember for long. The story breezed its way under the talking heads, "High School Senior Trapped Eight Months in Wisconsin Man's Basement." The name "Ruby Dowell" became another buzzword for news anchors and true crime enthusiasts to salivate over until their next meal. But it made its run, like most things, and then it quietly disappeared, leaving Ruby Dowell behind in obscurity like the rest of us.

Except she didn't.

A story was all it was for everyone else. An idea of a girl, an abstraction of an abduction. And that's a lot easier to play with than a person, than a real event. The image of a trapped girl doesn't quite sting the way a flesh-and-blood one does. And some asshole with access to a newspaper knew that.

Not long after I left my underground holding, some unknown indie band rose to stardom after the release of a song by a very familiar name. This was not a coincidence.

—

The New Yorker Hotel is a good place to hire a hooker. The whole place kind of looks like a hooker. The hotel's name blares across the top, temptingly red like a pair of cherry lips. It stands on the block gleaming with lights, demanding the attention of anyone who walks by. The taxi drops me off at the front.

The girl who lent me the stilettos gave me the room number. Room 433, a premium suite for the guests of honor. She wrote it down on a slip of paper, along with the shoes, while I slid her five-hundred bucks to cover the costs of her missing a gig.

My heels click on the marble floor as I make my way across the lobby. I try not to make too much noise. I tuck my coat closer, but it doesn't do much to hide me. Even if the coat hides the tight red dress, it can't hide my shoes or my lipstick and eyeshadow. The girl running the front desk keeps eyeing me.

I find an elevator and two minutes later I'm approaching Room 433. It's not hard to find, since there's a hulking man in a black t-shirt standing on the outside who watches me the whole walk down the hall.

"Can't let you in, sweetheart," he says. "The band's not seeing fans at the moment."

"I'm not a fan," I say. "I was asked to come here."

"Who's that, Anthony?"

The door behind the bodyguard opens, and a blonde candlestick of a boy pokes his head out. His eyes immediately fall to me, drink me in, staring at the opening of my coat the way a kid looks at Christmas wrapping paper.

"Oh, no worries," he tells the bodyguard. His eyes don't leave me. "This one's here on business."

Anthony looks at me for a second, then steps aside. The blonde, like a gentleman, opens the door for me to walk through.

"Gentlemen, we have a lady present," he calls into the living room.

In the living room, the two other members are seated on the couch. The drummer has his head bent over the table, his long black hair falling around his face. The lead guitarist has a brown fringe with his feet on the table and the guitar whining in his hands. Both look up at me when I walk in. Behind me, I hear the lead singer lock the door shut then take his place next to the others on the couch.

"You got a name?" the guitarist asks, like he's asking if I have a lighter on me. I don't lie to them.

"Ruby," I answer.

The guitarist looks at me for a second, chuckles, then looks over at the lead singer.

"Did you pay her to say that?" he asks. "This some kind of ego-trip for you?"

The lead singer laughs and gives him a shove.

"I swear, I had no idea what her name was," he says, then turns to me. "He thinks I asked you to call yourself after our song. Have you heard it?"

The way he says it lets me know it's not really a question. As if he expects me to say "Why no, I haven't heard the song that's been infesting the airwaves for months, the only one about *Ruby, Ruby red.*"

I smile and answer, "Yes I have."

"You like it?"

I know any negative answer is only going to turn them off, so I smile and nod my head in a way that makes my curls bounce.

"Yeah, I really like it," I say. And because I can't help it, "It reminds me of a lot of other songs."

The lead singer's smile doesn't go away, but his eyes dim. The drummer finally lifts his head and throws it over the back of the couch. There's blood in his nose and a sprinkle of white on the coffee table.

"Other songs?" the lead singer asks.

I shrug my shoulders innocently.

"It just reminds me of a lot of other songs," I say. "'Polly' by Nirvana. 'Jamie's Got A Gun' by Aerosmith. 'Sex Type Thing' by Stone Temple Pilots. Songs that imagine what it's like in the bad guy's head."

The drummer and guitarist just stare at me. The lead singer chuckles and pats me on the shoulder.

"I promise we're not like those bands, darling," he says. "Our sound is something new. Our next album is gonna innovate the rock genre as we know it." He leans over and grabs a can of Schweppes off the coffee table and takes a swig. He lets out a throaty *aww* then wipes his mouth on his flannel sleeve. "But I guess I can see the comparison. I wanted to get into the head of the villain. People like to make quick moral judgments, but I believe it's important to find the humanity in people who do bad things. Life's not always black-and-white."

I thought about the lines "*Ruby, sweet Ruby, girl.*" The nicest thing Jonas ever said to me was "drink this."

"This isn't poetry class," the guitarist says. "We're paying her to strip, not listen to your ramble about your supposed lyrical genius."

All three of them look at me. Even the coked-out drummer rolls his foggy eyes onto me. I finish unbuttoning my coat and open it just enough for them to a slit of red fabric.

"You three have been such nice hosts," I say. "Maybe I could repay with something?"

I walk over to a table in the corner. A tray with four glasses, and a half-empty bottle of scotch. I make sure to stick my rear out as I bend over to grab the tray. I contort my body as much as one can while I pour each of them a drink.

"I like this girl," the guitarist says behind me.

I keep my ass perked out so that's all they see. It's like a magic trick. You want to draw the audience's attention away from your hands so they don't see what you're doing. I reach into my coat pockets and pull out what I was looking for: Several tablets of fentanyl crunched to a fine powder. The high heels weren't the only thing that the girl at the club was so kind to offer.

I peek coyly over my shoulder. At least one of them is so out of it he'll barely notice. The other two, well, I don't think they're in their best minds either. The air in this apartment feels and smells powdery, and I doubt that white stuff on the table is the only thing they've managed to sneak past hotel security. Makes me wonder for a second if I just left now, they'd do the job for me.

But it's been nine months. That song is still stuck in my head, and I've long run out of patience waiting for it to go away. Just a few inches across the table where I stir the powder into the scotch, I see a Grammy, a Billboard music award, and an MTV music video award, all of them lined up nice and shiny.

The drinks are ready, and I take them over to the table. I lean down, ass out and tits barely staying in my dress, and set the tray before the boys. I grab mine and lift it in the air.

"Should we toast first?" I ask.

The boys don't object. They all cheer in a hardy "Heyyy!" and lift their glasses to mine. The old vinyl player pops, and scratches and a new song plays on the radio. It's another grunge song, with the distorted electric guitar and seedy drums. Our glasses clink together, and the boys lift them to their lips. I bring mine to my mouth, press my lips over the glass, and only allow the gold liquid to touch my upper lip, then I swallow some saliva. It's a trick I learned as a teen in church when Mama insisted I drink some of the communion wine even though I hated the yeasty taste.

"So are we doing this or what?" the guitarist asks. He says "we" like me taking off my clothes is a collaborative endeavor.

I give my sweetest smile, then lift my hand to one sleeve and bring it down my shoulder. The band watches with rapt attention as the song on the record player grows louder towards the chorus. By the time I have another sleeve peeled down, the drummer starts to cough. Between the cocaine and the fentanyl, it's not a shock that he's the first to go down. He collapses head-first onto the coffee table, his skull banging against the glass and making a mess of the cocaine. The other two laugh it off until they start coughing and notice the spill of vomit running down the table. The music is playing so loud I'm surprised they didn't get noise complaints.

"What the fuck?" the lead singer says. He watches as the guitarist collapses onto the floor, crunching inward and spewing bile from his lips. Then he looks at me. "What the fuck have you done?"

His eyes fall to the phone on the table. I snatch it up before he can take it, and I throw it against the wall. The thing shatters and bits of glass fall to the carpet. The lead singer rises from the couch and rushes at me but collapses into a fit of coughing and vomit.

"You...fucking bitch..." he spits through a mouthful of puke.

I look down at him. I remember the first time I got a good look at him was on the television. The Upgrade had won their first Grammy for best song. The boys had dolled up in tuxedos and threw their middle-fingers at the audience as they accepted their trophy for "Ruby," which had topped the billboards for weeks. No one remembered the name Ruby Dowell, but they would remember these three.

I watch him as he lies on his back on the floor. The messy slop drips down the side of his mouth. I say one last thing to him.

"My name is Ruby Dowell."

Three things cross his eyes: Confusion, something else, then nothing.

———

The 27 Club was an idea popularized in the late twentieth century. A series of great talents that died tragically young from the sex, drugs, and rock n' roll lifestyle. None of the members of The Upgrade were twenty-seven. They were twenty-two, twenty-five, and twenty-six respectively. None of them would ever have the luxury of joining Jimi Hendrix and Amy Winehouse in the VIP section in the sky. But that didn't make the tragedy of their deaths any less a spectacle.

The morning after, I see The Upgrade again, this time on a newspaper on a plastic stand at the door of the cafe across from my hotel. After the boys had laid still on the floor for a few minutes, I snuck out early that morning and told Anthony the boys had gone to bed. It wouldn't be until later that evening, when the boys were due to show up at the Apollo Theater, where people found them unmoving.

I read the paper over a plate of eggs and coffee. All politics and sports and dogs helping homeless people have been pushed aside in favor of overblown images of The Upgrade. Every newspaper on the stand is splattered with the same bold, black letters: RISING STARS FOUND DEAD IN THE NEW YORKER HOTEL.

The story plays out as any fan of Kurt Cobain would tell you. The Upgrade, an indie band at the top of their sudden shot to stardom, was found overdosed on cocaine and fentanyl in their hotel room before their performance at the Apollo Theater to a sold-out audience.

I let out a breath and took a long cup of coffee. There's music playing in the cafe, a soft woman's voice balloons over the few meager patrons. No distorted electric guitars, no seedy drums. I had managed to walk the block from my Airbnb to the cafe, ordered and waited for my breakfast, and finished my eggs, and I made it all that way without hearing *Ruby, Ruby red* anywhere. My head goes quiet, and I feel a smile waver onto my face.

Someone changes the channel on the television set on the wall. An anchorwoman's voice punctures my reverie.

"—this Friday. Fans everywhere are in mourning following the news that the music industry's favorite underdogs were sent to rest in their hometown cemetery in Wisconsin."

I glance over my shoulder at the television set. A series of pictures of the band flicks across the screen, followed by images of hordes of teenagers, red-eyed and snotty, weeping outside of Lenox Hill Hospital.

I roll my eyes and turn away from the television. Even in death, those boys still have to slather themselves over everything. I had my time with the talking heads. They get bored of people quickly.

"In honor of these fallen rock legends," the anchorwoman says. I snort. "We will be sharing the music video for the song that started it all. The 2019 hit single, 'Ruby.'"

I hear the opening drums and drop a couple of twenties on the table. I leave my half-finished coffee on top of the newspaper and leave the cafe.

The song muffles as I step out onto the street. But then I hear it again, in a car on the road, stuck in traffic with the windows rolled down and the radio playing full blast.

Asshole, I think, then speed faster down the sidewalk. I stop at a crosswalk, and the girl next to me has her music playing in her earbuds up to an ungodly volume. There it is again, that goddamn *Ruby, Ruby red.*

I'm walking so fast I don't even realize I passed my Airbnb and ended up in Times Square. The city is the loudest in this part. Too many people with earbuds blaring loud and jumbotrons screaming for my attention. I look up and there they are, The Upgrade shimmering across the skyscrapers like ghosts. Everyone within hearing distance of me is talking, and I hear all the same words in a cacophony.

The Upgrade...fentanyl...Ruby, Ruby red...gone and lost her head...

The city feels claustrophobic. I close my eyes and do what my therapist always told me to do. Deep breath, count to ten. But I can barely hear myself count with all the noise that crunches closer into me.

I only felt this cramped once before. A room buried under concrete and soil, dripping with mold and grime. A man standing at the top of the stairs, with something swirling in the red cup in his hand.

I lower myself onto a bench and let the noise wander over me.

The voices of The Upgrade wash over the city. Even in death, those boys won't shut up about *Ruby, Ruby red, gone and lost her head.*

I stand up and start walking home. The song crawls itself inside my head again, curling back in the space carved into its shape.

Ruby, Ruby red

Gone and lost her pretty head
Hear her down, down below
Hear her reap what I have sown

The Sandcastle

There was no doubt in my mind it was about to start raining, and the timing could not have been worse. I peered over the paperback on my lap. From the shore, I could see the dark skies swirling above the darkening waves. I looked to my left, then to my right. A few people were beginning to pack up their belongings and leave.

"Annabel," I said, shoving the book back into my beach bag. "I think we should go now."

My little sister looked up from her place on the ground by my feet. Her butt was half-buried in the sand and the rest of her body was dripping with saltwater. The clumpy, wet pile she called a sandcastle glopped in front of her.

"Can you at least let me finish it?" she pleaded, holding up the last touches of her masterpiece, clumps of thick wet sand oozing from her tiny toddler fists.

I stood up and began folding my beach chair.

"You can try," I said. "The rain will probably wash it away though."

Annabel hung her head down at her messy creation, not wanting to leave it.

"Come on," I said. "We need to get back to the house before the storm starts. I heard it might be a hurricane."

"Maybe we can get shelter inside the sandcastle."

"Don't be ridiculous."

I tried to grab her hand, but she cried out.

"Wait!" she said, then fished a tiny pink shell out from a tiny pocket in her swimsuit. "There's one more piece!"

I rolled my eyes and waited as she looked for a place to put it. I eyed nervously at the sky as a roll of thunder rumbled overhead.

She placed the pink shell just below the window of the front tower. The second it touched the sand, there was a snap, and I found myself flat on my face in the sand.

"What just…"

I lifted myself off the ground, and immediately didn't recognize where I was. The room was furnished with sofas, chairs, and even chandeliers, all of them glittering with gold. Except it wasn`t gold. It was sand.

I saw Annabel giggling and jumping in the corner.

"See Lee?" she chuckled. "I told you there would be room in the sandcastle for both of us! It'll protect us from the hurricane!"

I wanted to say something, but my dropped jaw was silent. I finally shook my head and gathered Annabel in my arms. We sat by the window, and watched the rain, and never once did the walls or roof of the sandcastle begin to dampen and fall.

It was hard to remember when the storm ended. It could have been minutes; it could have been days. All I remember was the sun peeking out from the clouds and glittering onto the waves. I looked down at Annabel. I was about to ask her how we got out of the sandcastle, but part of me didn't want to leave.

Annabel fished a pink shell from her pocket, the same one that brought us there in the first place and tightened it in her fist.

I blinked, and I was standing on the beach again. I was startled as the sun brushed against my skin and the seagulls chirped over-head. Annabel stood in front of me, hands on her hips and utterly pleased with herself.

"See," she said. "I told you there was room in the sandcastle."

Right next to her, the sandcastle was a pile of wet, sandy mush.

About the Author

Elizabeth Devido is currently pursuing a degree in creative writing at the University of North Carolina Asheville. When she's not writing, she enjoys theatre, daydreaming, and drinking excessive amounts of sweet iced tea. She lives in Wilmington, North Carolina.

www.ingramcontent.com/pod-product-compliance
Lightning Source LLC
Chambersburg PA
CBHW020732250626
47155CB00006B/2260